Knits for Everybody

by
Knit
Picks

Photography by Amy Cave

Printed in the United States of America

Second Printing, 2016

ISBN 978-1-62767-135-4

Versa Press, Inc

800-447-7829

www.versapress.com

CONTENTS

Introduction

Sometimes you just want to knit a simple project - nothing with fancy cables or complicated stitches - a classic that will fit almost everyone. Perhaps you've just discovered your love of knitting and you're ready to graduate from scarves to something a bit more challenging. Maybe you're an experienced knitter ready to begin customizing patterns to suit your unique style. No matter where you are on your knitting journey, *Knits for Everybody* has a project for you!

We chose four of our favorite basic knitting projects and created patterns in both fingering and worsted weight yarns. You'll find easy-to-understand instructions for each project in sizes ranging from newborn to men's XXL and women's plus sizes. *Knits for Everybody* includes a versatile top-down raglan sweater with a ribbed neck, cuffs, and hem, a beanie-style hat with simple decreases, a pair of socks (or slippers) with instructions for both top-down or toe-up knitting, and a sweet and easy pair of mittens.

Consider *Knits for Everybody* a handbook of basic patterns for the whole family. Whether you need a gift for a friend or family member, or you're knitting for yourself, there's a project on these pages for you. Grab your needles and favorite yarn, and cast on today!

HATS

by Joyce Fassbender

FINGERING WEIGHT

FINISHED MEASUREMENTS

10 (12, 14, 16, 18, 20, 22, 24)" circumference x 3.5 (4.5, 6, 7, 7.5, 8.5, 10, 11)" depth; to fit Preemie (Newborn, Baby, Toddler, Child, Teen, Adult, Large Adult)

YARN

Knit Picks Stroll (75% Superwash Merino Wool, 25% Nylon; 231 yards/50g): 1 skein. Shown in Dogwood Heather 25603 (14"), Duchess Heather 24594 (16"), Aurora Heather 25025 (22"), Sapphire Heather 24590 (24")

NEEDLES

US 3 (3.25mm) DPNs and 16" circular needle, or size to obtain gauge

NOTIONS

Yarn Needle
Stitch Markers

GAUGE

30 sts and 40 rnds = 4" in St st in the round, blocked

WORSTED WEIGHT

FINISHED MEASUREMENTS

10 (12, 14, 16, 18, 20, 22, 24)" circumference x 4 (4.75, 6.5, 7.25, 8.25, 9, 9.75, 11)" high; to fit Preemie (Newborn, Baby, Toddler, Child, Teen, Adult, Large Adult)

YARN

Knit Picks Swish Worsted (100% Superwash Merino Wool; 110 yards/50g): 1 (1, 1, 1, 1, 2, 2, 2) skeins. Shown in Peapod 25139 (14"), Honey 26066 (16"), Orange 25154 (22"), and Serrano 24663 (24")

NEEDLES

US 7 (4.5mm) DPNs and 16" circular needles, or size to obtain gauge

NOTIONS

Yarn Needle
Stitch Marker

GAUGE

20 sts and 26 rnds = 4" in St st in the rnd, blocked

For pattern support, contact joycef2@gmail.com

Fingering Weight Hat

Notes:

This hat is worked in the round from the bottom up.

In order to increase the depth of the hat, work additional rounds.

Use a stitch marker at the beginning of the round.

DIRECTIONS

Using a long-tail cast on, CO 64 (80, 92, 108, 124, 136, 148, 164) sts. PM and join in the rnd taking care not to twist.

Work Ribbing

Rnd 1: (K2, P2) rep 16 (20, 23, 27, 31, 34, 37, 41) times per rnd.

Repeat Rnd 1 until piece measures 1.5 (1.5, 2.5, 3, 3, 3.5, 4, 4)" from CO edge.

Each size, work one increase rnd:

10": (K1, KFB, P2) five times, (K2, P2) three times, (K1, KFB, P2) six times, (K2, P2) two times. (75 sts)

12": (K1, KFB, P2, K2, P2) ten times. (90 sts)

14": K1, KFB, P2, (K1, KFB, P2, K2, P2) five times, K1, KFB, P2, (K1, KFB, P2, K2, P2) five times, K1, KFB, P2. (105 sts)

16": K2, P2, (K1, KFB, P2, K2, P2) six times, K2, P2, (K1, KFB, P2, K2, P2) six times, K2, P2. (120 sts)

18": (K1, KFB, P2, K2, P2, K2, P2) nine times, (K1, KFB, P2, K2, P2) two times. (135 sts)

20": K2, P2, (K1, KFB, P2, K2, P2) seven times, (K2, P2) three times, (K1, KFB, P2, K2, P2) seven times, (K2, P2) two times. (150 sts)

22": K2, P2, (K1, KFB, P2, K2, P2) six times, K2, P2, (K1, KFB, P2, K2, P2) six times, K2, P2, (K1, KFB, P2, K2, P2) five times. (165 sts)

24": (K2, P2) three times, (K1, KFB, P2, K2, P2) six times, (K2, P2) three times, (K1, KFB, P2, K2, P2) five times, (K2, P2) three times, (K1, KFB, P2, K2, P2) five times. (180 sts)

Work Stockinette st Body

Rnd 1: K all sts.

Repeat Rnd 1 until piece measures 2.25, (3, 4, 4.75, 5, 5.5, 6.5, 7.25)" from CO edge.

Begin decreases.

Work Crown Decreases

Start working Crown decreases at rnd 26 (23, 20, 17, 13, 9, 5, 1). Switch to DPNs as needed.

Rnd 1: (K2tog, K10) fifteen times. (165 sts)

Rnds 2, 3, 4: K all sts.

Rnd 5: K5, (K2tog, K9) fourteen times, K2tog, K4. (150 sts)

Rnds 6, 7, 8: K all sts.

Rnd 9: (K2tog, K8) fifteen times. (135 sts)

Rnds 10, 11, 12: K all sts.

Rnd 13: K4, (K2tog, K7) fourteen times, K2tog, K3. (120 sts)

Rnds 14, 15, 16: K all sts.

Rnd 17: (K2tog, K6) fifteen times. (105 sts)

Rnds 18, 19: K all sts.

Rnd 20: K3, (K2tog, K5) fourteen times, K2tog, K2. (90 sts)

Rnds 21, 22: K all sts.

Rnd 23: (K2tog, K4) fifteen times. (75 sts)

Rnds 24, 25: K all sts.

Rnd 26: K2, (K2tog, K3) fourteen times, K2tog, K1. (60 sts)

Rnds 27, 28: K all sts.

Rnd 29: (K2tog, K2) fifteen times. (45 sts)

Rnds 30, 31: K all sts.

Rnd 32: (K1, K2tog) fifteen times. (30 sts)

Rnds 33, 34: K all sts.

Rnd 35: K2tog fifteen times. (15 sts)

Rnd 36: K all sts.

Rnd 37: K1, (K2tog seven times). (8 sts)

Rnd 38: K2tog four times. (4 sts)

Break yarn and run tail through remaining sts, pulling tightly to close.

Finishing

Weave in ends. Block and lay flat to dry.

Worsted Weight Hat

Notes:

The hat is worked in the round from the bottom up.

In order to increase the depth of the hat, work additional rounds of Stockinette st. Use a stitch marker at the beginning of the round.

DIRECTIONS

Using a long-tail cast on, CO 44 (56, 64, 72, 84, 88, 100, 108) sts. PM and join in the rnd taking care not to twist.

Work ribbing:

Rnd 1: (K2, P2), rep 11 (14, 16, 18, 21, 22, 25, 27) times per rnd.

Repeat Rnd 1 until piece measures 1.5 (1.5, 2.5, 2.5, 3, 3, 3, 4)" from CO edge.

Each size, work one increase rnd:

10": K1, KFB, P2, (K1, KFB, P2, K2, P2) four times, K2, P2, K1, KFB, P2. (50 sts)

12": K2, P2, (K1, KFB, P2, K2, P2, K2, P2) four times, K2, P2. (60 sts)

14": (K1, KFB, P2, K2, P2) three times, K2, P2, K2, P2, (K1, KFB, P2, K2, P2) three times, K2, P2, K2, P2. (70 sts)

16": K2, P2, (K1, KFB, P2, K2, P2) eight times, K2, P2. (80 sts)

18": (K2, P2) five times, (K1, KFB, P2, K2, P2) three times, (K2, P2) four times, (K1, KFB, P2, K2, P2) three times. (90 sts)

20": (K1, KFB, P2, K1, KFB, P2, K2, P2) three times, K2, P2, K2, P2, (K1, KFB, P2, K1, KFB, P2, K2, P2) three times, K2, P2, K2, P2. (100 sts)

22": (K1, KFB, P2, K2, P2) five times, (K2, P2) three times, (K1, KFB, P2, K2, P2) five times, K2, P2, K2, P2. (110 sts)

24": K2, P2, (K1, KFB, P2, K2, P2) six times, K2, P2, (K1, KFB, P2, K2, P2) six times, K2, P2. (120 sts)

Work Stockinette st body:

Rnd 1: K all sts.

Repeat Rnd 1 until piece measures 3 (3.5, 5, 5.5, 6, 6.5, 7, 8)" from CO edge.

Begin decreases.

Work Crown decreases:

Start working Crown decreases at rnd 15 (13, 11, 9, 7, 5, 3, 1). Switch to DPNs as needed.

Rnd 1: *K2tog, K10*, repeat * ten times. (110 sts)

Rnd 2: K all sts

Rnd 3: K5, *K2tog, K9*, repeat * nine times, K2tog, K4. (100 sts)

Rnd 4: K all sts

Rnd 5: *K2tog, K8*, repeat * ten times. (90 sts)

Rnd 6: K all sts

Rnd 7: K4, *K2tog, K7*, repeat * nine times, K2tog, K3. (80 sts)

Rnd 8: K all sts

Rnd 9: *K2tog, K6* repeat * ten times. (70 sts)

Rnd 10: K all sts

Rnd 11: K3, *K2tog, K5*, repeat * nine times, K2tog, K2. (60 sts)

Rnd 12: K all sts

Rnd 13: *K2tog, K4*, repeat * ten times. (50 sts)

Rnd 14: K all sts

Rnd 15: K2, *K2tog, K3*, repeat * nine times, K2tog, K1 (40 sts)

Rnd 16: K all sts

Rnd 17: *K2tog, K2*, repeat * ten times (30 sts)

Rnd 18: K all sts

Rnd 19: *K1, K2tog*, repeat * ten times (20 sts)

Rnd 20: *K2tog*, repeat * ten times (10 sts)

Rnd 21: *K2tog*, repeat * 5 times (5 sts)

Break yarn and run tail through remaining sts, pulling tightly to close.

Finishing

Weave in ends. Block and lay flat to dry.

MITTENS

by Jenny Williams

FINGERING WEIGHT

FINISHED MEASUREMENTS

3.75 (4.5, 5, 5.5, 5.75, 6, 6.5, 7.25, 7.75, 8.25, 8.75, 9.5)" hand circumference; sizes 5.5" to 9.5" are meant to be worn with .25" negative ease

YARN

Knit Picks Stroll (75% Superwash Merino Wool, 25% Nylon; 231 yards/50g): 1 (1, 1, 1, 1, 1, 1, 1, 1, 1, 2, 2) balls. Shown in Dogwood Heather 25603 (4.5"), Duchess Heather 24594 (5.5"), Sapphire Heather 24950 (7.25"), Aurora Heather 25025 (8.75")

NEEDLES

US 2 (3mm) DPNs or two 24" circular needles for two circulars technique, or one 32" or longer circular needle for Magic Loop technique, or size to obtain gauge

NOTIONS

Yarn Needle
Stitch Markers
Scrap Yarn or Stitch Holders

GAUGE

29 sts and 39 rows = 4" in St st in the rnd, blocked

WORSTED WEIGHT

FINISHED MEASUREMENTS

4 (4.5, 5, 5.25, 5.75, 6.5, 6.75, 7, 7.75, 8.25, 8.5, 9)" hand circumference; sizes 5.25 to 9" are meant to be worn with .25" negative ease

YARN

Knit Picks Swish Worsted (100% Superwash Merino Wool; 110 yards/50g): 1 (1, 1, 1, 1, 2, 2, 2, 2, 2, 2) balls. Shown in Peapod 25139 (4.5"), Honey 26066 (5.75"), Orange 24154 (7.75"), Serrano 24663 (8.25")

NEEDLES

US 6 (4mm) DPNs or two 24" circular needles for two circulars technique, or one 32" or longer circular needle for Magic Loop technique, or size to obtain gauge

US 5 (3.75mm) DPNs or two 24" circular needles for two circulars technique, or one 32" or longer circular needle for Magic Loop technique, or one size smaller than those used to obtain gauge

NOTIONS

Yarn Needle
Stitch Markers
Scrap Yarn or Stitch Holders

GAUGE

22.5 sts and 32 rows = 4" in St st in the rnd on larger needles, blocked

Fingering Weight Mittens

Notes:

These mittens are sized for babies through the largest adult. The gauge is intentionally a bit tight to produce a dense but elastic fabric. Knit in the rnd, they are worked from the ribbed cuff to the shaped mitten top, which is pulled or grafted shut, depending on size. Sizes 3.75" – 5" are thumb-less, for tiny hands. Sizes 5.5" – 9.5" are sized with .25" negative ease for a snug fit.

Tip:

After casting on, you may find it easier to work 2 – 3 rows flat before joining the sts to work in the rnd. It will make it easier to avoid twisting the sts. This tiny seam can be closed while finishing.

M1L (Make 1 Left-leaning stitch)

Slip the bar between st just worked and next st onto the LH needle, inserting LH needle under the bar from front to back. Knit through the back of the loop. The resulting st will be twisted which prevents it from making a hole.

M1R (Make 1 Right-leaning stitch)

Slip the bar between st just worked and next st onto the LH needle, inserting the LH needle tip from back to front. Knit through the front of the loop. The resulting st will be twisted which prevents it from making a hole.

K2, P2 Rib (worked in the rnd over multiples of 4 sts)

All Rnds: *K2, P2; rep from * to end of rnd.

Stockinette Stitch (St st, worked in the rnd over any number of sts)

All Rnds: Knit.

DIRECTIONS

Refer to Fingering Weight Mittens Chart and chose the size you want to knit. Apply the numbers for your selected size, which are provided in Rows A – V, to the corresponding blanks within the following pattern directions.

CO (A) __ sts. PM and join to work in the round, being careful not to twist sts. See Tip above.

Work in K2, P2 Rib for (B) __ " or desired length. Knit one rnd, placing marker after (C) __ sts, marking the midpoint or division between the front side and back side of the mitten.

Sizes 3.75 (4.5, 5)" ONLY: K (D) __" in St st and skip to Top Decreases.

All Other Sizes: K (D) __ rnds.

Mitten Body

Set Up Rnd: M1L (E) __ times, K to midpoint marker, SM, M1L (E) __ times, K to the end of the rnd. (F) __ sts.

Right Hand: K to midpoint marker, SM, K4, PM for gusset, M1L, K2, M1R, PM for gusset, K to end of rnd. 2 gusset sts inc.

Left Hand: K to 4 sts before midpoint marker, PM for gusset, M1L, K2, M1R, PM for gusset, K to end of rnd. 2 gusset sts inc.

Work Thumb Gusset

Rnd 1: K to 1st gusset marker, SM, M1L, K to next gusset marker, M1R, SM, K to end of rnd. 2 gusset sts inc.

Rnds 2, 3 and 4: Knit.

Work these four rnds (G) __ times total. On the next rnd, K to the first thumb gusset marker. Slip the (H) __ thumb sts onto stitch holder or scrap yarn, removing gusset markers. CO 2 sts onto RH needle. Join to next live st on LH needle and knit around the rest of the hand. (F) __ sts around the hand.

Work in St st for (I) __ ". On last rnd, K2tog (J) __ times, K to the midpoint marker, K2tog (J) __ times. (A) __ sts remain.

Top Decreases

(K2tog, K2) around. (K) __ sts remain. Work (L) __ rnds in St st.

(K2tog, K1) around. (M) __ sts remain. Work (N) __ rnds in St st.

K2tog around. (O) __ sts remain.

Sizes 3.75 to 6.5": Break yarn and, with a yarn needle, thread tail through remaining sts. Pull tight to close the hole.

Sizes 3.75 (4.5 and 5) ONLY: Proceed to Finishing.

Sizes 7.25 to 9.5": Work (P) __ rnds in St st. K2tog around. If 1 st remains, K1. (Q) __ sts remain. Break yarn and, with a yarn needle, thread tail through remaining sts. Pull tight to close the hole.

Thumb

Place the (H) __ held thumb sts back onto needles. Attach yarn and K 1 rnd. PU and K 4 sts over the gap. Join to work in the rnd. (R) __ total thumb sts.

Work in St st for (S) __ ".

Thumb Decreases

K2tog around. (T) __ sts remain. Work (U) __ rnds in St st.

K2tog around, if 1 st remains, K1. (V) __ sts remain.

Break yarn and, with a yarn needle, thread tail through remaining sts. Pull tight to close the hole.

Finishing

Weave in ends and close cuff seam, if you have one. Wash and block. Repeat for second mitten.

Worsted Weight Mittens

Notes:

These mittens are sized for babies through the largest adult. The gauge is intentionally a bit tight to produce a dense fabric. Knit in the rnd, they are worked from the ribbed cuff to the shaped mitten top, which is grafted shut. Sizes 4" to 5" are thumb-less, for tiny hands. Sizes 5.25" to 9" are sized with .25" negative ease for a snug fit.

Tip:

After casting on, you may find it easier to work 2 – 3 rows flat before joining the sts to work in the Rnd. It will make it easier to avoid twisting the sts. This tiny seam can be closed while finishing.

M1L (Make 1 Left-leaning stitch)

Slip the bar between st just worked and next st onto the LH needle, inserting needle tip from front to back. Knit through the back of the loop. The resulting st will be twisted which prevents it from making a hole.

M1R (Make 1 Right-leaning stitch)

Slip the bar between st just worked and next st onto the LH needle, inserting the needle tip from back to front. Knit through the front of the loop. The resulting st will be twisted which prevents it from making a hole.

K1, P1 Rib (in the rnd over multiples of 2 sts)

All Rnds: *K1, P1; rep from * to end of rnd.

Stockinette Stitch (St st, in the rnd over any number of sts)

All Rnds: Knit.

DIRECTIONS

Refer to Worsted Weight Mittens Chart and chose the size you want to knit. Apply the numbers for your selected size, which are provided in Rows A – Q, to the corresponding blank within the pattern directions.

With smaller needles, CO (A) ___ sts. PM and join to work in the round, being careful not to twist sts. See Tip above.

Work in K1, P1 Rib for (B) ___ " or desired length. Knit one rnd, placing marker after (C) ___ sts, marking the midpoint or division between the front side and back side of the mitten.

Change to larger needles and work (D) ___ rnds in St st. Note: For sizes 4, 4.5 and 5", skip to Top Decreases.

Thumb Gusset

Right Hand: K1, PM for gusset, M1L, K3, M1R, PM for gusset, K to end of rnd. 2 gusset sts inc.

Left Hand: K to 4 sts before midpoint marker, PM for gusset, M1L, K3, M1R, PM for gusset, K to end of rnd. 2 gusset sts inc.

Work Gusset

Rnds 1 and 2: Knit.
Rnd 3: Knit to 1st gusset marker, SM, M1L, K to next gusset marker, M1R, SM, K to end of rnd. 2 gusset sts inc.

Work these three rnds (E) ___ times total. (F) ___ total thumb sts.
Work (G) ___ rnds in St st.

Palm Increases

Rnd 1: K to 1 st before gusset marker, M1R, K1, SM, K to next gusset marker, SM, M1L, K to end of rnd. 2 palm sts inc.
Rnd 2: Knit.

Work (H) ___ rnds in St st.

On the next rnd, knit to the first thumb gusset marker. Slip the (F) ___ thumb sts onto stitch holders or scrap yarn, removing gusset markers. CO 3 sts onto RH needle, after last knit st on the hand. Join to next live st of the hand and knit around the rest of the hand. (I) ___ sts around the hand.

Work in St st for (J) ___ ".

Top Decreases

The top is shaped with decreases and grafted shut.

Rnd 1: K1, SSK, K to last 3 sts before side marker, K2tog, K1, SM; repeat for second side. 4 sts dec.
Rnd 2: Knit.

Work these 2 rnds (K) ___ times total. Work Rnd 1 once more. (L) ___ sts remain.

Break yarn and leave a tail long enough for grafting. With front mitten sts on first needle parallel to back mitten sts on second needle, graft front and back together, closing the top of the mitten. Note: Sizes 4, 4.5 and 5" skip to Finishing.

Thumb

Place the (F) ___ held thumb sts back onto larger needles. Attach yarn and knit 1 rnd. PU 3 sts across the 3 CO palm sts. Join to work in the rnd and place marker. (M) ___ total thumb sts.

Work in St st for (N) ___ ".

Thumb Decreases

Rnd 1: (K2tog, K2) around, if 2 sts remain, K2. (O) ___ sts remain.
Rnd 2: Knit.
Rnd 3: (K2tog, K1) around, if 2 sts remain, K2. (P) ___ sts remain.
Rnd 4: K2tog around. (Q) ___ sts remain.

Break yarn, leaving a 6" tail. With yarn needle, pass the yarn tail through the remaining sts and pull tight to close the hole. Pass tail to the WS through the top of the thumb.

Finishing

Weave in ends and close cuff seam, if you have one. Wash and block. Repeat for second mitten.

FINGERING WEIGHT MITTENS CHART

	Sizes	3.75"	4.5"	5"	5.5"	5.75"	6"	6.5"	7.25"	7.75"	8.25"	8.75"	9.5"
A	Cast on __ sts	28	32	36	40	40	44	48	52	56	60	64	68
B	Ribbing for ___"	1.25	1.5	1.75	2	2	2.25	2.5	2.5	2.75	2.75	3	3
C	PM after __ sts	14	16	18	20	20	22	24	26	28	30	32	34
D	Work ___" or rnds in St st	2.25	2.75	3.25	2	2	2	2	3	3	3	3	4
Mitten Body													
E	M1L ___ times	--	--	--	0	1	0	0	0	0	0	0	0
F	__ sts total	--	--	--	40	42	44	48	52	56	60	64	68
G	Work 4 thumb gusset rnds __ times total	--	--	--	5	6	7	8	8	8	9	9	10
H	__ total thumb sts	--	--	--	14	16	18	20	20	20	22	22	24
I	Work in St st for __"	--	--	--	1.75	2.5	3	3	3	3.5	3.5	4	4
J	K2TOG __ times	--	--	--	0	1	0	0	0	0	0	0	0
Top Decreases													
K	K2TOG, K2 around. __ sts remain	21	24	27	30	30	33	36	39	42	45	48	51
L	Work __ rnds in St st	0	0	0	2	2	2	3	3	3	3	3	3
M	K2 TOG, K1 around. __ sts remain	14	16	18	20	20	22	24	26	28	30	32	34
N	Work __ rnds in St st	0	0	0	2	2	2	3	3	3	3	3	3
O	K2TOG around. __ sts remain	7	8	9	10	10	11	12	13	14	15	16	17
P	Work __ rnds in St st	--	--	--	--	--	--	--	2	2	2	2	2
Q	K2TOG around. __ sts remain	--	--	--	--	--	--	--	7	7	8	8	9
Thumb													
R	__ total thumb sts	--	--	--	18	20	22	24	24	24	26	26	28
S	Work St st for __"	--	--	--	1.25	1.5	1.75	2	2.5	2.75	3	3	3.25
Thumb Decreases													
T	K2TOG around. __ sts remain	--	--	--	9	10	11	12	12	12	13	13	14
U	Work __ rnds in St st	--	--	--	0	0	0	2	2	2	2	2	3
V	K2TOG around. __ sts remain	--	--	--	5	5	6	6	6	6	7	7	7

WORSTED WEIGHT MITTENS CHART

	Sizes	4"	4.5"	5"	5.25"	5.75"	6.5"	6.75"	7"	7.75"	8.25"	8.5"	9"
A	Cast on __ sts	22	26	28	28	30	34	36	38	42	44	46	48
B	Ribbing for __"	1.25	1.5	1.75	2	2	2.25	2.5	2.5	2.75	2.75	3	3
C	PM after __ sts	11	13	14	14	15	17	18	19	21	22	23	24
D	Work __ rnds in St st	24	28	32	2	2	2	2	3	3	3	3	4
Thumb Gusset													
E	Work 3 thumb gusset rnds __ times total	--	--	--	3	3	3	4	4	4	4	5	5
F	__ total thumb sts	--	--	--	11	11	11	13	13	13	13	15	15
G	Work __ rnds in St st	--	--	--	2	2	2	2	2	2	2	2	2
Palm Increases													
H	Work __ rnds in St st	--	--	--	1	1	1	2	2	2	2	2	2
I	__ sts around the hand	22	26	28	30	32	36	38	40	44	46	48	50
J	Work in St st for __"	--	--	--	1.75	2.25	3	3.5	3.5	3.75	4	4.25	4.75
Top Decreases													
K	Work 2 dec rnds __ times total	2	3	3	4	4	4	4	4	5	5	5	5
L	__ remaining sts to graft tog	10	10	12	10	12	16	18	20	20	22	24	26
Thumb													
M	__ total thumb sts	--	--	--	14	14	14	16	16	16	16	18	18
N	Work St st for __"	--	--	--	1	1.5	1.75	2	2.5	2.75	3	3	3.25
Thumb Decreases													
O	Rnd 1: __ sts remain	--	--	--	11	11	11	12	12	12	12	14	14
P	Rnd 3: __ sts remain	--	--	--	8	8	8	8	8	8	8	10	10
Q	Rnd 4: __ sts remain	--	--	--	4	4	4	4	4	4	4	5	5

SOCKS AND SLIPPERS

by Allison Griffith

FINGERING WEIGHT

FINISHED MEASUREMENTS

4 (4.5, 5, 5.5, 6, 6.5, 7, 7.5, 8, 8.5, 9, 9.5, 10)" foot and leg circumference; sock is meant to be worn with zero or slight negative ease

YARN

Knit Picks Stroll (75% Superwash Merino Wool, 25% Nylon; 231 yards/50g): Shown in Dandelion 25024 (4"), Mint 27235 (6"), and Dogwood Heather 25603 (8"); 1 (1, 1, 1, 1, 2, 2, 2, 2, 2, 2, 2, 2) balls

NEEDLES

US 2 (2.75mm) DPNs, or size to obtain gauge

NOTIONS

Stitch Marker (for top-down socks)
Yarn Needle

GAUGE

32 sts and 40 rows = 4" in St st worked in the round, blocked

WORSTED WEIGHT

FINISHED MEASUREMENTS

4.5 (5, 5.75, 6.5, 7.25, 8, 8.75, 9.5, 10.25)" foot circumference; slipper is meant to be worn with zero or slight negative ease

YARN

Knit Picks Swish Worsted Yarn (100% Superwash Merino Wool; 110 yards/50g): Shown in Honey 26066 (4"), Wonderland Heather 26067 (6"), and Dove Heather 25631 (8"); 1(1, 1, 2, 2, 2, 2, 2, 2) balls

NEEDLES

US 5 (3.75mm) DPNs, or size to obtain gauge

NOTIONS

Stitch Marker (for top-down slippers)
Yarn Needle

GAUGE

22 sts and 32 rows = 4" in St st worked in the round, blocked

For pattern support, contact knittingontheneedles@gmail.com

Fingering Weight Socks

Notes:

These simple socks can be knit from the top down, or the toe up with virtually the same results. Try both, and decide which feels best for you!

Judy's Magic Cast On

Follow the instructions provided on the Knit Picks website here: http://tutorials.knitpicks.com/wptutorials/judys-magic-cast-on/

Kitchener Stitch

Follow the instructions provided on the Knit Picks website here: http://tutorials.knitpicks.com/wptutorials/kitchener-stitch/

Wrap and Turn (W&T)

Work until the stitch to be wrapped. If knitting: bring yarn to the front of the work, slip next st as if to purl, return the yarn to the back; turn work and slip wrapped st onto RH needle. Continue across row. If purling: bring yarn to the back of the work, slip next st as if to purl, return the yarn to the front; turn work and slip wrapped st onto RH needle. Continue across row.

Picking up wraps: Work to the wrapped st. If knitting, insert the RH needle under the wrap(s), then through the wrapped st K-wise. Knit the wrap(s) together with the wrapped st. If Purling, slip the wrapped st P-wise onto the RH needle, and use the LH needle to lift the wrap(s) and place them on the RH needle. Slip wrap(s) and unworked st back to LH needle; purl all together through the back loop.

2 x 2 Rib (worked in the rnd over multiples of 4 sts)
All Rnds: *K2, P2; rep from * around.

DIRECTIONS
Top Down Socks
Leg

Loosely CO 32 (36, 40, 44, 48, 52, 56, 60, 64, 68, 72, 76, 80), Distribute sts evenly across 4 needles being careful not to twist, PM and join to work in the rnd.
Work in 2 x 2 Rib around for 2.5 (3, 4, 4, 4.5, 5, 5, 5.5, 5.5, 5.5, 6, 6, 6)" or desired leg length.
K 2 rnds.

Heel Flap

Work the following 2 rows 8 (9, 10, 11, 12, 13, 14, 15, 16, 17, 18, 19, 20) times, working back and forth, ending with Row 2:
Row 1 (RS): Sl 1, K 15 (17, 19, 21, 23, 25, 27, 29, 31, 33, 35, 37, 39), turn.
Row 2 (WS): Sl 1, P 15 (17, 19, 21, 23, 25, 27, 29, 31, 33, 35, 37, 39), turn.

Turn Heel

Work the following 2 rows to set up heel turn:
Row 1 (RS): K 8 (9, 10, 11, 12, 13, 14, 15, 16, 17, 18, 19, 20), PM, K2, K2tog, K1, W&T.
Row 2 (WS): P to marker, SM, P2, P2tog, P1, W&T.
Continue, working the following 2 rows 0 (1, 1, 1, 2, 2, 2, 3, 3, 3, 4, 4, 4) times, ending with Row 2. (If 0, omit this step and proceed directly to Gusset.)

Row 1: K to 1 before the W&T gap (SM as you pass it), K2tog, K1, W&T.

Row 2: P to 1 before the W&T gap (SM as you pass it), P2tog, P1, W&T.

Gusset

Set up gusset as follows, working in the rnd:
K across the heel flap, SM as you pass it. Using the same needle, PU 8 (9, 10, 11, 12, 13, 14, 15, 16, 17, 18, 19, 20) sts along the side of the heel flap. This is Needle 1.

K across the top of the foot, using the next 2 needles (these are Needles 2 and 3).

Using your spare needle, PU 8 (9, 10, 11, 12, 13, 14, 15, 16, 17, 18, 19, 20) sts along the remaining side of the heel flap, then K to the marker. This is Needle 4. Remove marker.

Needles 1 and 4 (sole of foot) should have 15 (16, 18, 20, 21, 23, 25, 26, 28, 30, 31, 33, 35) sts. Needles 2 and 3 (top of foot) should have 8 (9, 10, 11, 12, 13, 14, 15, 16, 17, 18, 19, 20) sts.

Work the following 2 rnds 7 (7, 8, 9, 9, 10, 11, 11, 12, 13, 13, 14, 15) times, ending with Round 2.

Round 1: Needle 1: K to 2 sts before end, K2tog. Needle 2 and 3: K. Needle 4: Ssk, K to end.
Round 2: K. 32 (36, 40, 44, 48, 52, 56, 60, 64, 68, 72, 76, 80) sts.

Foot

Work even in St st (K all sts) until foot measures about 3 (3.25, 3.5, 4, 4.5, 5.5, 6.5, 7, 7.5, 7.75, 8.5, 8.5, 8.75)" from back of heel, or 1 (1.25, 1.5, 1.5, 1.5, 1.75, 1.75, 2, 2.25, 2.25, 2.5, 2.5, 2.75)" less than desired foot length.

Toe

Work the following rounds 5 (6, 7, 7, 8, 9, 9, 10, 11, 11, 12, 13, 14) times, ending with Round 2.

Round 1: Needle 1: K to 2 sts before end, K2tog. Needle 2: Ssk, K to end. Needle 3: K to 2 sts before end, K2tog. Needle 4: Ssk, K to end.
Round 2: K. 12 (12, 12, 16, 16, 16, 20, 20, 20, 24, 24, 24, 24) sts.

Finishing

Use the Kitchener st to close the toe. Weave in any remaining ends and block.

Toe-Up Socks
Toe

With Judy's Magic Cast On, CO 12 (12, 12, 16, 16, 16, 20, 20, 20, 24, 24, 24, 24) sts evenly over 2 needles. PM for beginning of rnd.
Work the following two rnds 5 (6, 7, 7, 8, 9, 9, 10, 11, 11, 12, 13, 14) times. Round 1: K.
Round 2: *K1, M1L, K to 1 st before end of needle, M1R, K1; rep from * once more. 32 (36, 40, 44, 48, 52, 56, 60, 64, 68, 72, 76, 80) sts.

Foot

Divide the sts evenly among 4 needles. Needles 1 and 2 are now the sole of the foot, needles 3 and 4 are now the top of the foot. Work even in St st (K all sts) until sock measures about 1.5 (2, 2.25, 2.5, 2.75, 3.75, 4.5, 5, 5.5, 5.5, 6, 6, 6)" from the tip of toe, or until sock measures 2.5 (2.5, 2.75, 3, 3.25, 3.5, 4, 4, 4.5, 4.75, 4.75, 5, 5.5)" less than desired foot length.

Gusset

Work the following 2 rounds 7 (7, 8, 9, 9, 10, 11, 11, 12, 13, 13, 14, 15) times, ending with Round 2.

Round 1: Needle 1: K1, M1L, K to end. Needle 2: K to 1 st before end, M1R, K1. Needles 3 and 4: K.

Round 2: K. 46 (50, 56, 62, 66, 72, 78, 82, 88, 94, 98, 104, 110) sts.

Turn Heel

Work the following 2 rows to set up heel. (Note: Heel is worked back and forth.)

Row 1 (RS): Needle 1: K to end. Needle 2: K 4 (4, 5, 6, 6, 7, 8, 8, 9, 10, 10, 11, 12), KFB, K1, W&T.

Row 2 (WS): Needle 2: P to end. Needle 1: P 4 (4, 5, 6, 6, 7, 8, 8, 9, 10, 10, 11, 12), PFB, P1, W&T.

Continue, working the following 2 rows 0 (1, 1, 1, 2, 2, 2, 3, 3, 3, 4, 4, 4) times. (If 0, omit this step and proceed directly to Heel Flap.)

Row 1 (RS): Needle 1: K to end. Needle 2: K to 6 sts before W&T gap, KFB, K1, W&T.

Row 2 (WS): Needle 2: P to end. Needle 1: P to 6 sts before W&T gap, PFB, P1, W&T. 48 (54, 60, 66, 72, 78, 84, 90, 96, 102, 108, 114, 120) sts.

Heel Flap

Work the following 2 rows to set up heel flap, continuing to work back and forth:

Row 1 (RS): Needle 1: K to end. Needle 2: K 7 (8, 9, 10, 11, 12, 13, 14, 15, 16, 17, 18, 19), picking up wraps as you go, Ssk, turn.

Row 2 (WS): Sl 1, P 14 (16, 18, 20, 22, 24, 26, 28, 30, 32, 34, 36, 38), working across Needles 2 and 1, and picking up wraps as you go, P2tog, turn.

Continue, working the following 2 rows until 32 (36, 40, 44, 48, 52, 56, 60, 64, 68, 72, 76, 80) sts remain, ending with Row 2.

Row 1 (RS): Sl 1, K 14 (16, 18, 20, 22, 24, 26, 28, 30, 32, 34, 36, 38), Ssk, turn.

Row 2 (WS): Sl 1, P 14 (16, 18, 20, 22, 24, 26, 28, 30, 32, 34, 36, 38), P2tog, turn.

Leg

Resume working in the round, knitting all sts for 2 rnds.

Work in 2 x 2 Rib until the leg measures 2.5 (3, 4, 4, 4.5, 5, 5, 5.5, 5.5, 5.5, 6, 6, 6)", or desired length.

Finishing

BO loosely.

Weave in any remaining ends and block.

Worsted Weight Slippers

Notes:

These simple slippers can be knit from the top down, or the toe up with virtually the same results. Try both and decide which feels best for you!

Judy's Magic Cast On

Follow the instructions provided on the Knit Picks website here: http://tutorials.knitpicks.com/wptutorials/judys-magic-cast-on/

Kitchener Stitch

Follow the instructions provided on the Knit Picks website here: http://tutorials.knitpicks.com/wptutorials/kitchener-stitch/

Wrap and Turn (W&T)

Work until the stitch to be wrapped. If knitting: bring yarn to the front of the work, slip next st as if to purl, return the yarn to the back; turn work and slip wrapped st onto RH needle. Continue across row. If purling: bring yarn to the back of the work, slip next st as if to purl, return the yarn to the front; turn work and slip wrapped st onto RH needle. Continue across row.

Picking up wraps: Work to the wrapped st. If knitting, insert the RH needle under the wrap(s), then through the wrapped st K-wise. Knit the wrap(s) together with the wrapped st. If purling, slip the wrapped st P-wise onto the RH needle, and use the LH needle to lift the wrap(s) and place them on the RH needle. Slip wrap(s) and unworked st back to LH needle; purl all together through the back loop.

2 x 2 Rib (worked in the rnd over multiples of 4 sts)

All Rnds: *K2, P2; rep from * to end of rnd.

DIRECTIONS
Top Down Slippers

Leg

CO 24 (28, 32, 36, 40, 44, 48, 52, 56). Distribute sts evenly across 4 needles, PM and join to work in the rnd being careful not to twist.

Work in 2 x 2 Rib around for .5 (.5, 1, 1, 1.5, 1.5, 2, 2)" or desired length.

K 2 rounds.

Heel Flap

Work the following 2 rows 6 (7, 8, 9, 10, 11, 12, 13, 14) times, working back and forth, ending with Row 2:

Row 1 (RS): Sl 1, K 11 (13, 15, 17, 19, 21, 23, 25, 27), turn.

Row 2 (WS): Sl 1, P 11 (13, 15, 17, 19, 21, 23, 25, 27), turn.

Turn Heel

Work the following 2 rows to set up heel turn:

Row 1 (RS): K 6 (7, 8, 9, 10, 11, 12, 13, 14), PM, K2, K2tog, K1, W&T.

Row 2 (WS): P to marker, SM, P2, P2tog, P1, W&T.

Continue, working the following 2 rows 0 (0, 0, 1, 1, 1, 2, 2, 2) times, ending with Row 2. (If 0, omit this step and proceed directly to Gusset.)

Row 1: K to 1 st before the W&T gap (SM as you pass it), K2tog, K1, W&T.

Row 2: P to 1 st before the W&T gap (SM as you pass it), P2tog, P1, W&T.

Gusset

Set up gusset as follows, working in the round:
K across the heel flap, SM as you pass it. Using the same needle, PU 6 (7, 8, 9, 10, 11, 12, 13, 14) sts along the side of the heel flap. This is Needle 1.

K across the top of the foot, using the next 2 needles (these are Needles 2 and 3).

Using your spare needle, PU 6 (7, 8, 9, 10, 11, 12, 13, 14) sts along the remaining side of the heel flap, then K to the marker. This is Needle 4. Remove marker.

Needles 1 and 4 (sole of foot) should have 11 (13, 15, 16, 18, 20, 21, 23, 25) sts. Needles 2 and 3 (top of foot) should have 6 (7, 8, 9, 10, 11, 12, 13, 14) sts.

Work the following 2 rnds 5 (6, 7, 7, 8, 9, 9, 10, 11) times, ending with Round 2.
Round 1: Needle 1: K to 2 sts before end, K2tog. Needle 2 and 3: K. Needle 4: Ssk, K to end
Round 2: K. 24 (28, 32, 36, 40, 44, 48, 52, 56) sts.

Foot

Work even in St st (K all sts) until foot measures about 3 (4, 4.75, 6, 6.75, 7.25, 8, 8.75, 9.25)" from back of heel, or 1 (1, 1.25, 1.5, 1.75, 1.75, 2, 2.25, 2.25)" less than desired foot length.

Toe

Work the following rnds 4 (4, 5, 6, 7, 7, 8, 9, 9) times, ending with Round 2.
Round 1: Needle 1: K to 2 sts before end, K2tog. Needle 2: Ssk, K to end. Needle 3: K to 2 sts before end, K2tog. Needle 4: Ssk, K to end.
Round 2: K. 8 (12, 12, 12, 12, 16, 16, 16, 20) sts.

Finishing

Use the Kitchener st to close the toe.
Weave in any remaining ends and block.

Toe-Up Slippers

Toe

With Judy's Magic Cast On, CO 8 (12, 12, 12, 12, 16, 16, 16, 20) sts evenly over 2 needles. PM for beginning of rnd.

Work the following two rnds 4 (4, 5, 6, 7, 7, 8, 9, 9) times.
Round 1: K.
Round 2: *K1, M1L, K to 1 st before end of needle, M1R, K1; rep from * once more. 24 (28, 32, 36, 40, 44, 48, 52, 56) sts.

Foot

Divide the sts evenly among 4 needles. Needles 1 and 2 are now the sole of the foot, needles 3 and 4 are now the top of the foot.

Work even in St st (K all sts) until slipper measures about 1.5 (2.25, 2.75, 4, 4.5, 4.75, 5.5, 6, 6.25)" from the tip of toe, or until slipper measures 2.25 (2.75, 3.25, 3.5, 3.75, 4.25, 4.5, 4.75, 5.25)" less than desired foot length.

Gusset

Work the following 2 rnds 5 (6, 7, 7, 8, 9, 9, 10, 11) times, ending with Round 2.
Round 1: Needle 1: K1, M1L, K to end. Needle 2: K to 1 st before end, M1R, K1. Needles 3 and 4: K.
Round 2: K. 34 (40, 46, 50, 56, 62, 66, 72, 78) sts.

Turn Heel

Work the following 2 rows to set up heel. (Note: Heel is worked back and forth.)
Row 1 (RS): Needle 1: K to end. Needle 2: K 2 (3, 4, 4, 5, 6, 6, 7, 8,), KFB, K1, W&T.
Row 2 (WS): Needle 2: P to end. Needle 1: P 2 (3, 4, 4, 5, 6, 6, 7, 8,), PFB, P1, W&T.

Continue, working the following 2 rows 0 (0, 0, 1, 1, 1, 2, 2, 2) times. (If 0, omit this step and proceed directly to Heel Flap.)
Row 1 (RS): Needle 1: K to end. Needle 2: K to 6 sts before W&T gap, KFB, K1, W&T.
Row 2 (WS): Needle 2: P to end. Needle 1: P to 6 sts before W&T gap, PFB, P1, W&T. 36 (42, 48, 54, 60, 66, 72, 78, 84) sts.

Heel Flap

Work the following 2 rows to set up heel flap, continuing to work back and forth:
Row 1 (RS): Needle 1: K to end. Needle 2: K 5 (6, 7, 8, 9, 10, 11, 12, 13), picking up wraps as you go, Ssk, turn.
Row 2 (WS): Sl 1, P 10 (12, 14, 16, 18, 20, 22, 24, 26), working across Needles 2 and 1, and picking up wraps as you go, P2tog, turn.

Continue, working the following 2 rows until 24 (28, 32, 36, 40, 44, 48, 52, 56) sts remain, ending with Row 2.
Row 1 (RS): Sl 1, K 10 (12, 14, 16, 18, 20, 22, 24, 26), Ssk, turn.
Row 2 (WS): Sl 1, P 10 (12, 14, 16, 18, 20, 22, 24, 26), P2tog, turn.

Leg

Resume working in the rnd, knitting all sts for 2 rnds.
Work 2 x 2 Rib until the leg measures .5 (.5, 1, 1, 1.5, 1.5, 2, 2)", or desired length.

Finishing

BO loosely.
Weave in any remaining ends and block.

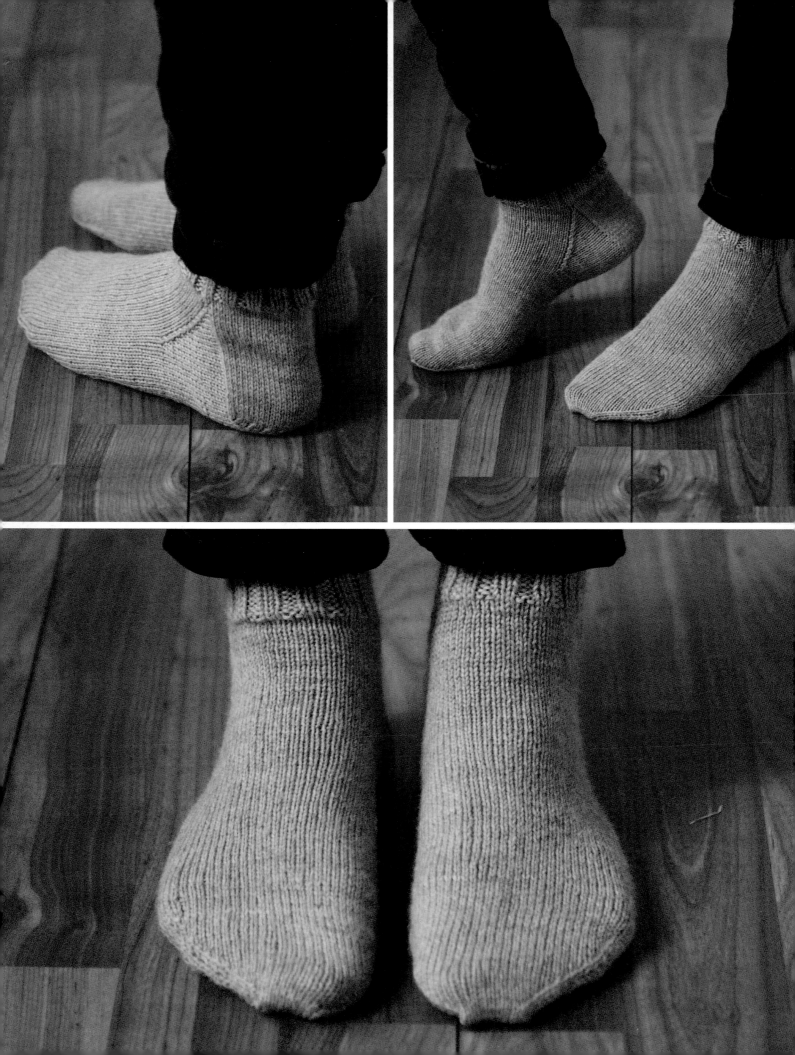

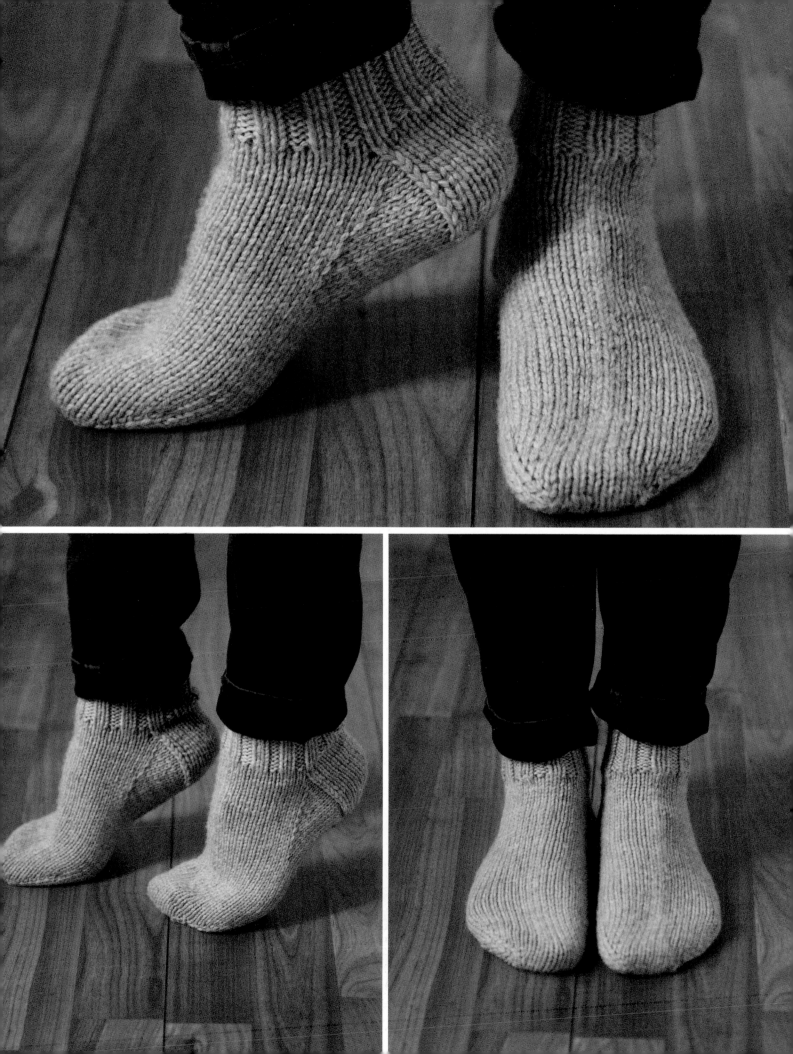

Fingering Weight Sweater

Notes:

This pattern is written for a wide range of sizes. To make pattern reading easier, the numbers (st counts, number of reps, etc.) have been placed in a chart with one column per size. The written pattern has blank spaces labeled with letters which correspond to the row of the chart where you can find the number you need. If you see "—" instead of a number, you will skip the corresponding instructions. Before beginning, you may want to read through the pattern and pencil in all of the numbers for your size in their corresponding spaces. The Number Chart can be found on the pages after the instructions.

Right-leaning Lifted Increase (RLI)

RS: Insert right needle tip from behind and under into the st below the first st on the left needle and lift it onto the left needle and K it.

WS: Insert the left needle tip from the front into the st 2 sts below the first st on the right needle and P.

Left-leaning Lifted Increase (LLI)

RS: Insert left needle tip from behind and under into the st 2 sts below the first st on the right needle and lift it up and K it.

WS: Insert right needle tip from the front into the st below the first st on the left needle and lift it onto the left needle and PTBL.

1x1 Rib (in the round over an even number of sts)

Every Rnd: * K1, P1, rep from * to the end of rnd.

Invisible Ribbed Bind-off

Measure out a tail of yarn three times the length of 1x1 Rib you are binding off and thread it on a yarn needle. Insert the yarn needle P-wise through the first (K) st and pull through, leaving the st on the needle. Insert the yarn needle K-wise through the next (P) st and pull the yarn through, leaving the st on the needle. * Insert the yarn needle K-wise through the first K st and pull the yarn through, letting the st fall off the needle. Insert the yarn needle P-wise into the next K st and pull the yarn through. Insert the yarn needle P-wise into the first P st and pull the yarn through, letting the st fall off the needle. Bring the yarn needle behind the first K st and insert it K-wise into the next P st, pulling the yarn through. Repeat from * until one st remains. Pull the yarn through this st and fasten off.

DIRECTIONS

Yoke

The yoke is worked back and forth until the neck shaping is completed and the piece is joined to work in the round.

There are two types of inc rows and three types of inc rnds referenced in the yoke shaping. Each is defined below.

8-St Inc Row (RS): * K to 1 st before marker, RLI, K1, SM, K1, LLI, rep from * three times more, K to the end. 8 sts inc; 1 in each front, 2 in each sleeve, and 2 back sts.

8-St Inc Row (WS): * P to 1 st before marker, LLI, P1, SM, P1, RLI, rep from * three times more, P to the end. 8 sts inc; 1 in each front, 2 in each sleeve, and 2 back sts.

8-St Inc Rnd: * K1, LLI, K to 1 st before marker, RLI, K1, SM, rep from * to the end. 8 sts inc; 1 in each front, 2 in each sleeve, and 2 back sts.

Sleeve-only Inc Rnd: * K1, LLI, K to 1 st before marker, RLI, K1, SM, K to marker, SM, rep from * to the end. 4 sts inc; 2 in each sleeve.

Body-only Inc Rnd: * K to marker, SM, K1, LLI, K to 1 st before marker, RLI, K1, SM, rep from * to the end. 4 sts inc; 2 front and 2 back sts.

With larger needle, CO (A)_____ sts.

Next Row (WS): P1 right front st, PM, P2 right sleeve sts, PM, P (B)_____ back sts, PM, P2 left sleeve sts, PM, P1 left front st. Read ahead as Yoke and Neck Shaping are worked simultaneously.

Yoke Shaping

Beginning on the RS, work the appropriate 8-St Inc Row every row (C)_____ times. You may find it easier to work M1s on the initial Inc Row. Then work the 8-St Inc Row every RS row (D)_____ times.

Neck Shaping

At the same time, begin shaping the neck edge. After (E)_____ rows, inc 1st at each neck edge every RS row 4 times.

At the beginning of the next 2 rows, CO (F)_____ sts.
At the beginning of the next (RS) row, CO (G)_____ center front sts. 206 (206, 210, 210, 218, 218, 218, 218, 218, 218, 246, 246, 238, 258, 258, 262, 294, 298, 318, 318, 322, 258, 278, 318, 322, 322) sts on needles.

Work an 8-St Inc Row, then join to work in the rnd. PM to denote beginning of rnd. Yoke shaping continues in the round. Work the 8-St Inc Rnd every rnd (H)_____ times, then every other rnd (I)_____ times. Then work the Sleeve-only Inc Rnd every rnd (J)_____ times. Then work the Body-only Inc Rnd every rnd (K)_____ times. 250 (266, 282, 298, 314, 302, 326, 350, 370, 386, 398, 414, 426, 410, 446, 482, 530, 582, 614, 702, 746, 458, 502, 558, 606, 654) sts on needles.

Separating Body and Sleeves

Remove beginning of rnd marker. K to the next marker and remove it. Place (L)_____ left sleeve sts on scrap yarn or stitch holder. CO (M)_____ underarm sts, PM in the middle of these for new beginning of rnd. If you have no CO, PM between the front and back. K across (N)_____ back sts, remove marker. Place (M)_____ right sleeve sts on scrap yarn or st holder. Remove marker, CO (M)_____ underarm sts, if working Waist Shaping PM in the middle of these. K across (N)_____ front sts. K to the end. 142 (150, 158, 166, 174, 178, 194, 210, 222, 234, 250, 262, 270, 250, 282, 314, 346, 374, 406, 438, 470, 498, 282, 310, 342, 374, 406) sts on needles. Rnds now begin and end at the left side.

Body

The body is worked straight down to the hem. Optional waist shaping instructions are provided for Youth and Women's sizes; if you choose to make waist shaping, skip the next sentence. Continue straight until the body measures (O)_____ inches from the underarm CO, or (V) inches less than desired body length.

Waist Shaping

For Youth and Women's sizes only: If you opt for waist shaping, continue straight until the body measures (P)_____ inches from the underarm CO.

Waist Dec Rnd: * K1, SSK, K to 3 sts before marker, K2tog, K1, SM, rep from * to the end. 4 sts dec.

Work the Waist Dec Rnd every (Q)_____ rnds (R)_____ times total. (S)_____ sts dec. Continue straight until body measures (T)_____ inches from the underarm CO.

Waist Inc Rnd: * K1, LLI, K to 1 st before marker, RLI, K1, SM, rep from * to the end. 4 sts inc.

Work the Waist Inc Rnd every (U)_____ rnds (S)_____ times total. (S) sts inc. Continue straight until body measures (O)_____ inches from underarm CO, or (V) inches less than desired body length.

Continue for all sizes.

Hem

Change to smaller needles and work 1x1 Rib for (V)_____ inches. BO using the Invisible Rib Bind-off.

Sleeves

Perform these instructions for each sleeve. Return (L)_____ sleeve sts to larger needles. Join yarn to the center of the underarm CO. If you have no CO, join yarn to where the front and back are joined. PU and K (W)_____ underarm sts along the underarm CO edge, K the sleeve sts, PU and K (W)_____ underarm sts along the underarm CO edge, PM for beginning of the rnd.

Sleeve Dec Rnd: * K1, SSK, K to 3 sts before the end, K2tog, K1. 2 sts dec.

Work the Sleeve Dec Rnd every (X)_____ rnds (Y)_____ times. (Z)_____ sts on needles. Continue straight until sleeve measures (AA)_____ inches from underarm CO, or (V) inches less than desired length.

Cuff

Change to smaller needles and work 1x1 Rib for (V)_____ inches. BO using the Invisible Rib Bind-off.

Finishing

Weave in ends, wash and block to schematic.

Neckband

Join yarn to the neck opening between the back and the left sleeve. With smaller needles and RS facing, PU and K around the neck opening at a rate of 1 st for each CO st and 4 sts for every 5 rows. Adjust st count as needed to achieve an even number of sts.

Work 1x1 Rib for (AB)_____ inches.
BO using the Invisible Rib Bind-off.

Worsted Weight Sweater

Notes:

This pattern is written for a wide range of sizes. To make pattern reading easier, the numbers (st counts, number of reps, etc.) have been placed in a chart with one column per size. The written pattern has blank spaces labeled with letters which correspond to the row of the chart where you can find the number you need. If you see "--" instead of a number, you will skip the corresponding instructions. Before beginning, you may want to read through the pattern and pencil-in all of the numbers for your size in their corresponding spaces. The Number Chart can be found immediately following the written instructions.

Right-leaning Lifted Increase (RLI)

RS: Insert right needle tip from behind and under into the st below the first st on the left needle and lift it onto the left needle and K it.

WS: Insert the left needle tip from the front into the st 2 sts below the first st on the right needle and P.

Left-leaning Lifted Increase (LLI)

RS: Insert left needle tip from behind and under into the st 2 sts below the first st on the right needle and lift it up and K it.

WS: Insert right needle tip from the front into the st below the first st on the left needle and lift it onto the left needle and PTBL.

1x1 Rib (in the round over an even number of sts)

Every Rnd: * K1, P1, rep from * to the end of rnd.

Invisible Ribbed Bind-off

Measure out a tail of yarn three times the length of 1x1 Rib you are binding off and thread it on a yarn needle. Insert the yarn needle P-wise through the first (K) st and pull through, leaving the st on the needle. Insert the yarn needle K-wise through the next (P) st and pull the yarn through, leaving the st on the needle. * Insert the yarn needle K-wise through the first K st and pull the yarn through, letting the st fall off the needle. Insert the yarn needle p-wise into the next K st and pull the yarn through. Insert the yarn needle P-wise into the first P st and pull the yarn through, letting the st fall off the needle. Bring the yarn needle behind the first K st and insert it K-wise into the next P st, pulling the yarn through. Repeat from * until one st remains. Pull the yarn through this st and fasten off.

DIRECTIONS
Yoke

The yoke is worked back and forth until the neck shaping is completed and the piece is joined to work in the round.

There are two types of increase rows and three types of increase rnds referenced in the yoke shaping. Each is defined below.

8-St Inc Row (RS): * K to 1 st before marker, RLI, K1, SM, K1, LLI, rep from * three times more, K to the end. 8 sts inc; 1 in each front, 2 in each sleeve, 2 back sts.

8-St Inc Row (WS): * P to 1 st before marker, LLI, P1, SM, P1, RLI, rep from * three times more, P to the end. 8 sts inc; 1 in each front, 2 in each sleeve, 2 back sts.

8-St Inc Rnd: * K1, LLI, K to 1 st before marker, RLI, K1, SM, rep from * to the end. 8 sts inc; 2 in the front, 2 in each sleeve, 2 back sts.

Sleeve-only Inc Rnd: * K1, LLI, K to 1 st before marker, RLI, K1, SM, K to marker, SM, rep from * to the end. 4 sts inc; 2 in each sleeve.

Body-only Inc Rnd: * K to marker, SM, K1, LLI, K to 1 st before marker, RLI, K1, SM, rep from * to the end. 4 sts inc; 2 front and 2 back sts.

With larger needle, CO (A)_____ sts.

Next Row (WS): P1 right front st, PM, P2 right sleeve sts, PM, P (B)_____ back sts, PM, P2 left sleeve sts, PM, P1 left front st. Read ahead as Yoke and Neck Shaping are worked simultaneously.

Yoke Shaping

Beginning on the RS, work the appropriate 8-St Inc Row every row (C)_____ times. You may find it easier to work M1s on the initial Inc Row. Then work the 8-St Inc Row every RS row (D)_____ times.

Neck Shaping

At the same time, begin shaping the neck edge. After (E)_____ rows, inc 1st at each neck edge every RS row (F)_____ times.

At the beginning of the next 2 rows, CO (G)_____ sts.
At the beginning of the next (RS) row, CO (H)_____ center front sts. 130 (130, 130, 138, 122, 138, 138, 138, 130, 122, 142, 134, 126, 138, 146, 162, 178, 198, 206, 238, 238, 242, 154, 154, 166, 182, 198) sts on needles.

Work 8-St Inc Row, then join to work in the rnd. PM to denote beginning of rnd. Yoke shaping continues in the round. Work the 8-St Inc Rnd every rnd (I)_____ times, then every other rnd (J)_____ times, then every 4 rnds (K)_____ times. Then work the Sleeve-only Inc Rnd every rnd (L)_____ times. Then work the Body-only Inc Rnd every rnd (M)_____ times. 162 (170, 178, 190, 198, 206, 214, 222, 230, 242, 258, 266, 274, 254, 282, 310, 338, 374, 394, 450, 474, 506, 290, 322, 354, 382, 414) sts on needles.

Separating Body and Sleeves

Remove beginning of rnd marker. K to the next marker and remove it. Place (N)_____ left sleeve sts on scrap yarn or stitch holder. CO (O)_____ underarm sts, PM before the center st of these CO sts to mark the new beginning of rnd. K across (P)_____ back sts, remove marker. Place (N)_____ right sleeve sts on scrap yarn or st holder. Remove marker, CO (O)_____ underarm sts, if working Waist Shaping PM in the middle of these, or before CO st if only 1 st is CO. K across (P)_____ front sts. K to the end. 92 (96, 100, 104, 108, 116, 124, 136, 140, 148, 160, 168, 172, 160, 180, 200, 220, 240, 260, 280, 300, 320, 180, 200, 220, 240, 260) sts on needles. Rnds now begin and end at the left side.

Body

The body is worked straight down to the hem. Optional waist shaping instructions are provided for Youth and Women's sizes; if you choose to make waist shaping, skip the next sentence.

Continue straight until the body measures (Q)_____ inches from the underarm CO, or (W) inches less than desired body length.

Waist Shaping

For Youth and Women's sizes only: if you opt for waist shaping, continue straight until the body measures (R)_____ inches from the underarm CO.

Waist Dec Rnd: * K1, SSK, K to 3 sts before marker, K2tog, K1, SM, rep from * to the end. 4 sts dec.
Work the Waist Dec Rnd every (S)_____ rnds 5 times total. 20 sts dec.
Continue straight until body measures (T)_____ inches from the underarm CO.

Waist Inc Rnd: * K1, LLI, K to 1 st before marker, RLI, K1, SM, rep from * to the end. 4 sts inc.
Work the Waist Inc Rnd every (U)_____ rnds 5 times total. 20 sts inc.

Continue straight until body measures (Q)_____ inches from underarm CO or (V) inches less than desired body length. Continue for all sizes.

Hem

Change to smaller needles and work 1x1 Rib for (V)_____ inches. BO using the Invisible Rib Bind-off.

Sleeves

Perform these instructions for each sleeve. Return (N)_____ sleeve sts to larger needles. Join yarn to the center of the underarm CO. PU and K (W)_____ underarm sts along the underarm CO edge, K the sleeve sts, PU and K (W)_____ underarm sts along the underarm CO edge, PM for beginning of the rnd.

Sleeve Dec Rnd: * K1, SSK, K to 3 sts before the end, K2 tog, K1. 2 sts dec.
Work the Sleeve Dec Rnd every (X)_____ rnds (Y)_____ times. (Z)_____ sts on needles. Continue straight until sleeve measures (AA)_____ inches from underarm CO, or (W) inches less than desired length.

Cuff

Change to smaller needles and work 1x1 Rib for (V)_____ inches. BO using the Invisible Rib Bind-off.

Finishing

Weave in ends, wash and block to schematic.

Neckband

Join yarn to the neck opening between the back and the left sleeve. With smaller needles PU and K around the neck opening at a rate of 1 st for each CO st and 4 sts for every 5 rows. Adjust st count as needed to achieve an even number of sts. Work 1x1 Rib for (AB)_____ inches. BO using the Invisible Rib Bind-off.

FINGERING WEIGHT SWEATER CHART

	Baby					Child					Youth			Woman									Man				
	3 mo	6 mo	12 mo	18 mo	24 mo	2	4	6	8	10	12	14	16	XS	S	M	L	1X	2X	3X	4X	5X	S	M	L	XL	XXL
A	36	36	38	38	42	42	42	42	42	42	42	42	42	44	44	46	46	48	48	50	50	52	48	50	50	52	52
B	30	30	32	32	36	36	36	36	36	36	36	36	36	38	38	40	40	42	42	44	44	46	42	44	44	46	46
C	17	18	18	18	18	17	18	18	18	18	20	20	17	22	22	22	26	26	26	28	28	28	14	18	28	28	28
D	1	--	--	--	--	1	--	--	--	--	1	1	3	--	--	--	--	--	--	--	--	--	7	5	--	--	--
E	8	8	8	8	8	8	8	8	8	8	12	12	12	12	12	12	16	16	16	18	18	18	18	18	18	18	18
F	3	3	3	3	4	4	4	4	4	4	4	5	5	5	5	6	6	6	6	7	7	7	6	7	7	7	7
G	14	14	16	16	18	18	18	18	18	18	18	16	16	18	18	18	18	20	20	20	20	22	20	20	20	22	22
H	--	--	1	1	1	--	--	4	5	3	--	--	--	--	4	6	10	18	20	35	42	46	--	--	1	8	14
I	1	3	3	5	5	6	10	10	12	17	18	20	17	16	16	12	12	10	8	5	2	2	22	26	27	26	24
J	7	7	8	8	10	7	5	3	2	--	--	--	--	2	--	--	--	--	--	--	--	--	4	2	2	--	--
K	--	--	--	--	--	--	--	--	--	--	2	4	5	--	5	9	13	13	21	14	17	19	--	--	--	1	5
L	56	60	64	68	72	66	70	74	78	80	80	82	84	86	88	92	100	112	112	140	148	156	98	106	120	128	136
M	--	--	--	--	--	2	2	2	2	2	6	6	6	6	6	8	8	8	8	8	10	10	10	10	12	12	12
N	70	74	78	82	86	86	94	102	108	114	118	124	128	118	134	148	164	178	194	210	224	238	130	144	158	174	190
O	4.75	5.5	5.75	6	5.75	6	6.5	7.5	9	10	11.5	12.5	13.5	16	16	15.75	15.5	15.25	15	14.5	14.5	14	18.5	19.5	19.5	19.5	19.5
P	--	--	--	--	--	--	--	--	--	--	--	--	--	4	4	4	4.25	4.25	4.25	4.75	4.75	--	--	--	--	--	--
Q	--	--	--	--	--	--	--	--	--	--	8	7	7	10	10	9	8	8	8	6	6	6	--	--	--	--	--
R	--	--	--	--	--	--	--	--	--	--	4	5	5	5	5	5	5	5	5	5	5	5	5	5	6	6	6
S	--	--	--	--	--	--	--	--	--	--	16	20	20	20	20	20	20	20	20	20	20	20	--	--	--	--	--
T	--	--	--	--	--	--	--	--	--	--	7	7	7	10	10	9.75	9.5	9.25	9	8.5	8.5	8	--	--	--	--	--
U	--	--	--	--	--	--	--	--	--	--	7	7	9	8	8	8	8	8	8	8	8	8	--	--	--	--	--
V	1	1	1	1	1.5	1.5	1.5	1.5	1.5	1.5	1.75	1.75	1.75	2	2	2	2	2	2	2	2	2	2.5	2.5	2.5	2.5	2.5
W	--	--	--	--	--	1	1	1	1	1	3	3	3	3	3	4	4	4	4	4	5	5	5	5	6	6	6
X	13	13	14	15	16	12	12	12	12	11	11	12	11	12	13	12	11	6	10	5	5	4	13	11	8	7	6
Y	13	13	14	15	16	12	12	12	12	11	12	12	13	13	12	13	15	17	17	30	35	38	13	16	23	26	29
Z	32	36	38	40	42	46	50	54	58	62	62	64	64	66	70	74	78	86	86	88	88	90	82	84	86	88	90
AA	5.5	6	7	7.5	8.25	8.25	10.25	11.5	12.5	13.5	15.25	16.25	16.5	17.5	18	18	18.5	18.5	19	19	19.5	19.5	19.5	20	21	21.5	22
AB	0.5	0.5	0.5	0.5	0.5	0.5	0.5	0.5	0.5	0.5	0.75	0.75	0.75	1	1	1	1	1	1	1	1	1	1	1	1	1	1

WORSTED WEIGHT SWEATER CHART

	Baby					Child					Youth			Woman									Man				
	3 mo	6 mo	12 mo	18 mo	24 mo	2	4	6	8	10	12	14	16	XS	S	M	L	1X	2X	3X	4X	5X	S	M	L	XL	XXL
A	25	25	25	25	29	29	29	29	29	29	31	31	31	33	33	33	33	35	35	35	35	37	37	37	39	39	39
B	19	19	19	19	23	23	23	23	23	23	25	25	25	27	27	27	27	29	29	29	29	31	31	31	33	33	33
C	6	6	6	7	3	5	5	5	3	2	3	1	--	1	4	7	10	14	15	22	22	22	--	--	1	6	10
D	5	5	5	5	6	6	6	6	7	7	8	9	9	9	7	6	5	3	3	--	--	--	11	11	11	8	6
E	5	5	5	5	6	6	6	6	7	7	8	9	9	9	7	6	5	3	3	--	--	4	11	11	11	8	6
F	3	3	3	3	3	4	4	4	4	4	4	4	4	4	4	4	4	4	4	4	4	4	4	4	4	4	4
G	2	2	2	2	2	2	2	2	2	2	3	3	3	3	3	3	2	3	3	2	2	3	3	3	3	3	3
H	7	7	7	7	9	9	9	9	9	9	9	9	9	11	11	11	13	13	13	15	15	15	15	15	17	17	17
I	--	--	--	--	--	--	--	--	--	--	--	--	--	--	--	--	--	--	--	2	4	9	--	--	--	--	--
J	1	2	3	3	5	5	7	9	11	14	13	14	16	13	15	15	15	17	16	19	19	17	10	17	21	24	25
K	--	--	--	--	--	--	--	1	1	--	--	--	--	--	--	--	--	--	--	--	--	--	4	2	3	--	--
L	4	4	4	5	7	5	3	3	3	3	5	3	3	1	2	5	8	8	13	9	11	12	4	2	3	--	2
M	--	--	--	--	--	--	--	--	--	--	1	3	3	--	--	5	8	8	13	9	11	12	--	--	--	--	2
N	36	38	40	44	46	46	46	46	48	50	52	52	54	52	56	60	64	72	72	90	94	100	62	68	76	80	86
O	1	1	1	1	1	1	1	3	3	3	3	3	3	5	5	5	5	5	5	5	7	7	7	7	9	9	9
P	45	47	49	51	53	57	61	65	67	71	77	81	83	75	85	95	105	115	125	135	143	153	83	93	101	111	121
Q	4.75	5.75	6	6.25	5.75	6	6.5	7.5	9.25	10.25	11.5	12.75	13.75	16	16	16	15.75	15.25	15	14.5	14.5	14.25	18.5	19.5	19.5	19.5	19.5
R	--	--	--	--	--	--	--	--	--	--	3.5	3.5	3.5	4	4	4	4	4	4	4	4	4	4	4	5	--	--
S	--	--	--	--	--	--	--	--	--	--	6	6	6	8	8	7	7	7	6	5	5	5	8	8	7	5	5
T	--	--	--	--	--	--	--	--	--	--	7.5	8	8	10	10	9.75	9.5	9.25	9	8.5	8.5	8	--	--	--	--	--
U	--	--	--	--	--	--	--	--	--	--	4	5	7	8	8	8	8	8	8	8	8	8	--	--	--	--	--
V	1	1	1	1	1.5	1.5	1.5	1.5	1.5	1.5	1.75	1.75	1.75	2.25	2.25	2.25	2.25	2.25	2.25	2.25	2.25	2.25	2.5	2.5	2.5	2.5	2.5
W	1	1	1	1	1	1	1	2	2	2	2	2	2	3	3	3	3	3	3	3	4	4	4	4	5	5	5
X	4	5	6	5	6	6	9	12	13	14	14	17	15	16	17	15	13	12	12	7	6	5	16	13	10	9	8
Y	9	8	8	10	10	8	8	7	7	7	8	7	8	8	8	9	10	11	11	20	23	25	9	11	15	17	19
Z	20	24	26	26	28	30	32	36	38	40	40	42	42	42	46	48	50	56	56	56	56	58	52	54	56	56	58
AA	5.5	6.25	7	7.5	8.25	8.25	10.25	11.5	12.5	13.5	15.25	16.25	16.75	17.5	18.25	18.25	18.5	18.5	19	19	19.5	19.5	19.5	20	21	21.5	22.25
AB	0.5	0.5	0.5	0.5	0.5	0.5	0.5	0.5	0.5	0.5	0.75	0.75	0.75	1	1	1	1	1	1	1	1	1	1	1	1	1	1

FINGERING WEIGHT SWEATER SCHEMATIC MEASUREMENTS

		Baby					Child					Youth		
	Sizes	3 mo	6 mo	12 mo	18 mo	24 mo	2	4	6	8	10	12	14	16
A	Chest/Bust	18	19	20.25	21.25	22.25	22.75	24.75	26.75	28.5	30	32	33.5	34.5
B	Waist	--	--	--	--	--	--	--	--	--	--	30	31	32
C	Upper Arm	7.25	7.75	8.25	8.75	9.25	8.75	9.25	10	10.5	10.75	11	11.25	11.5
D	Wrist	4	4.75	5	5.25	5.5	6	6.5	7	7.5	8	8	8.25	8.25
E	Front Neck Drop	2.5	2.25	2.25	2.25	2.25	2.5	2.25	2.25	2.25	2.25	2.75	2.75	2.75
F	Armhole Length	3.75	4	4	4.5	4.75	4.75	5.25	5.5	5.75	6.5	7	7.25	8
G	Body Length	5.75	6.75	7	7.25	7.25	7.5	8	9	10.75	11.75	13.25	14.5	15.5
H	Sleeve Length	6.5	7	8	8.5	9.75	9.75	11.75	13	14	15	17	18	18.25

CON'T FINGERING WEIGHT SWEATER SCHEMATIC MEASUREMENTS

		Woman									Man				
	Sizes	XS	S	M	L	1X	2X	3X	4X	5X	S	M	L	XL	XXL
A	Chest/Bust	32	36.25	40.25	44.5	48	52.25	56.25	60.5	64	36.25	39.75	43.75	48	52.25
B	Waist	29.5	33.5	37.75	41.75	45.5	49.5	53.75	57.75	61.5	--	--	--	--	--
C	Upper Arm	12	12	13	14	15.5	15.5	19	20.5	21.5	14	15	17	18	19
D	Wrist	8.5	9	9.5	10	11	11	11.25	11.25	11.5	10.5	10.75	11	11.25	11.5
E	Front Neck Drop	2.75	2.75	2.75	3.25	3.25	3.25	3.25	3.25	3.25	3.25	3.25	3.25	3.25	3.25
F	Armhole Length	7	7.25	8	8.5	8.75	9.5	10	10.5	11	8.75	9.5	9.75	10.25	10.75
G	Body Length	18.25	18.25	8.25	18	17.5	17.25	16.75	16.75	16.5	21	22	22	22	22
H	Sleeve Length	19.5	20	20	20.5	20.5	21	21	21.5	21.5	22	22.5	23.5	24	24.5

WORSTED WEIGHT SWEATER SCHEMATIC MEASUREMENTS

		Baby					Child					Youth		
	Sizes	3 mo	6 mo	12 mo	18 mo	24 mo	2	4	6	8	10	12	14	16
A	Chest/Bust	18.5	19.25	20	20.75	21.5	23.25	24.75	27.25	28	29.5	32	33.5	34.5
B	Waist	--	--	--	--	--	--	--	--	--	--	28	29.5	30.5
C	Upper Arm	7.5	8	8.5	9.25	9.5	9.5	9.5	10	10.5	10.75	11.25	11.25	11.5
D	Wrist	4	4.75	5.25	5.25	5.5	6	6.5	7.25	7.5	8	8	8.5	8.5
E	Front Neck Drop	2.25	2.25	2.25	2.5	2.25	2.5	2.5	2.5	2.5	2.25	2.75	2.75	2.5
F	Armhole Length	3.5	3.75	4	4.75	5	5.25	5.75	6.5	6.75	7.25	7.5	6.75	7.25
G	Body Length	5.75	6.75	7	7.25	7.25	7.5	8	9	10.75	11.75	13.25	14.5	15.5
H	Sleeve Length	6.5	7.25	8	8.5	9.75	9.75	11.75	13	14	15	17	18	18.5

CON'T WORSTED WEIGHT SWEATER SCHEMATIC MEASUREMENTS

		Woman									Man				
	Sizes	XS	S	M	L	1X	2X	3X	4X	5X	S	M	L	XL	XXL
A	Chest/Bust	32	36	40	44	48	52	56	60	64	36	40	44	48	52
B	Waist	28	32	36	40	44	48	52	56	60	--	--	--	--	--
C	Upper Arm	11.5	12.5	13.25	14	15.5	15.5	19.25	20.5	21.5	14	15.25	17.25	18	19.25
D	Wrist	8.5	9.25	9.5	10	11.25	11.25	11.25	11.25	11.5	19.5	10.75	11.25	11.25	11.5
E	Front Neck Drop	2.75	2.5	2.75	2.75	2.75	3	3	3	3	3	3	3.25	3	3
F	Armhole Length	7.75	8.25	8.75	9.25	9.75	10.5	10.75	8.75	9.25	9.5	9.75	10.5	10.25	10.75
G	Body Length	18.25	18.25	18.25	18	17.5	17.25	16.75	16.75	16.5	21	22	22	22	22
H	Sleeve Length	19.75	20.5	20.5	20.75	20.75	21.25	21.25	21.75	21.75	22	22.5	23.5	24	24.75

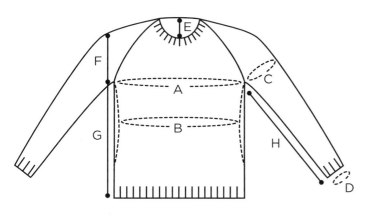

HOW TO TAKE MEASUREMENTS

Taking accurate measurements is important for good fit. Measure over underwear that you'd usually wear under your garments, and hold the measuring tape a tiny bit loose.

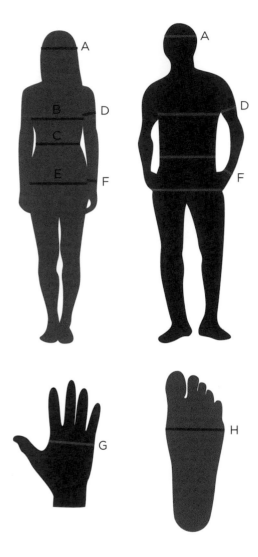

A. Head: Measure around forehead, just above the eyebrow

B. Chest/Bust: Measure at the widest part of the chest for men and children, bust for women.

C. Waist: Measure at the smaller point of the midsection, slightly above the belly button.

D. Upper Arm: Measure around the upper arm, close to the armpit.

E. Hip: Measure around the widest part of the hips.

F. Wrist: Measure around by the wrist bone.

G. Hands: Measure around the widest part of the palm.

H. Feet: Measure around the wideest part of the foot.

PERSONALIZATION IDEAS

Adding a few inches onto the cuffs or borders of a garment to lengthen it for tall people, or to give a garment a slouchy look.

Add fancy buttons for decoration to hats and sweaters.

Use contrasting colors for different parts of the garment. For example, make the cuffs a bright color and the body a dark color.

Use two or more colors for stripes. Vary the stripes' width.

Colorblock a garment.

Use different ribbing stitches, like twisted ribbing, for a subtle change.

Purl a row every so often for a textural stripe pattern.

Use a different border stitch for cuffs and hems, such as garter stitch instead of 1x1 ribbing.

Hold two contrasting strands of yarn together for a marled look.

Sew your gauge swatch onto the front of a garment for a pocket.

If you're in between sizes, using a gauge that's 1 stitch more than called for can give a slightly bigger size, and 1 less than called for can give a slightly smaller size.

Make extra-extra large slippers out of 100% wool (not superwash!) and felt them to your size.

Use yarn scraps to embroider designs onto mittens, hats, and sweaters.

Abbreviations							
BO	bind off	M	marker		stitch	TBL	through back loop
cn	cable needle	M1	make one stitch	RH	right hand	TFL	through front loop
CC	contrast color	M1L	make one left-leaning	rnd(s)	round(s)	tog	together
CDD	Centered double dec		stitch	RS	right side	W&T	wrap & turn (see
CO	cast on	M1R	make one right-lean-	Sk	skip		specific instructions
cont	continue		ing stitch	Sk2p	sl 1, k2tog, pass		in pattern)
dec	decrease(es)	MC	main color		slipped stitch over	WE	work even
DPN(s)	double pointed	P	purl		k2tog: 2 sts dec	WS	wrong side
	needle(s)	P2tog	purl 2 sts together	SKP	sl, k, psso: 1 st dec	WYIB	with yarn in back
EOR	every other row	PM	place marker	SL	slip	WYIF	with yarn in front
inc	increase	PFB	purl into the front and	SM	slip marker	YO	yarn over
K	knit		back of stitch	SSK	sl, sl, k these 2 sts tog		
K2tog	knit two sts together	PSSO	pass slipped stitch	SSP	sl, sl, p these 2 sts tog		
KFB	knit into the front and		over		tbl		
	back of stitch	PU	pick up	SSSK	sl, sl, sl, k these 3 sts		
K-wise	knitwise	P-wise	purlwise		tog		
LH	left hand	rep	repeat	St st	stockinette stitch		
		Rev St st	reverse stockinette	sts	stitch(es)		

Knit Picks yarn is both luxe and affordable—a seeming contradiction trounced! But it's not just about the pretty colors; we also care deeply about fiber quality and fair labor practices, leaving you with a gorgeously reliable product you'll turn to time and time again.

THIS COLLECTION FEATURES

STROLL
Fingering Weight
75% Superwash Merino Wool,
25% Nylon

SWISH WORSTED
Worsted Weight
100% Superwash Merino Wool

View these beautiful yarns and
more at www.KnitPicks.com